Krishna
Photocopies Himself

by

Nishita Chaitanya

 C·H·I·N·M·A·Y·A B·A·L·A K·A·T·H·A

It was a bright and beautiful day.

All the little boys were happy. They were happy to be with Krishna. Krishna was the funniest, cleverest, strongest, bravest and kindest little blue boy there ever was.

Krishna and his friends had taken the little calves out to the forest. The calves grazed on the lovely green grass.

The little boys looked after the calves to make sure nothing happened to them. Their fathers took care of the big cows, and the boys looked after the little calves.

The calves were munching and munching on the grass for hours and hours. And all day long, they moo-moooooed. Krishna and his friends got a little tired watching them.

Krishna had an idea. "Let's play a game," he said to the other boys. And so they did. They played hide and seek. They played catch and tag. They played duck duck goose. They played so many games, and had so much fun.

All the playing and watching the calves munching and munching and munching, and mooing and mooing and mooing, made the cowherd boys hungry.

They found a big shady tree with sweet-smelling white flowers. Under the tree, they sat in a circle to have their lunch.

Everyone wanted to sit next to Krishna.

So Krishna sat in the center of the circle, where he was close to everyone.

While eating, they told jokes which made them laugh and laugh. They were having so much fun that they forgot all about the calves.

Uh-oh!

"Oh, no! Where are the calves? They must have wandered away," said one of Krishna's worried friends.

"This is terrible! Our fathers will be angry at us," said another of Krishna's fretting friends.

"What shall we do, Krishna? What shall we do?" said a third, very VERY worried friend.

"Don't worry," said Krishna, "I shall find the cows and bring them back. You keep eating. It will not take me long." And Krishna walked away to find the missing calves.

"Thank goodness for Krishna, he is such a good friend," the boys said to each other.

"We never have to worry about anything when Krishna is with us... . Yes, never. Krishna takes care of everything," all the boys agreed.

Krishna walked for a while following the calves' footprints, but he could not find the animals.

He walked and walked, but he just could not find them. He walked further towards the hills, but he still could not find them. He could not find the calves anywhere.

"This is surprising," thought Krishna. "Where could they have gone?"

He thought maybe his friends could help him search for the calves. So he walked back towards the forest brook.

When he got to the brook, he looked under the big shady tree, but "Oh! No!" his friends were not there.

Not here, not there, not anywhere!

STRANGE! First the cows went missing, and now his friends had disappeared!

What was going on?

Krishna could see everything in the whole wide world. He could see everything that had happened, and everything that was going to happen.

So Krishna closed his eyes and looked inside to understand what had happened on this bright and beautiful day in the forest.

Up above in the sky, on a fluffy white cloud, sat an old old man. He had long white hair, a long white moustache and a long white beard. He was a wise angel called Brahma.

Every day and every night he watched. He watched the sky, and the rivers, and the birds, and the flowers, and the grass, and the animals, and the people. He watched everything and everyone. He was even watching Krishna.

He had seen Krishna drive away many big and powerful demons before. He had seen Krishna save people from spells and curses, from trouble and suffering. But most of all, he had seen how everyone loved Krishna so much.

Brahma stroked his long white beard as he thought, "Hmmm, can this little boy really be so strong? Could he be more powerful than me? I should test him. I shall play a game with him, to show him how wise and mighty I am."

So while Krishna and his friends were eating, Brahma came down from his fluffy white cloud in the big blue sky and used his magic to put all the calves to sleep.

He then hid all the calves in a deep dark cave. When Krishna went to look for the calves, Brahma used his magic again to put all of Krishna's friends to sleep. Then he hid them, too.

But remember, **Krishna knows everything**.

He looked within himself and found out what had happened: "Oh! This wise angel is playing hide and seek."

Krishna knows where to seek. He knows everything. He could have found his friends and calves and woken them up right away.

But Krishna just smiled, because...

...because he had a better idea, a MUCH better idea!

Krishna photocopied himself twenty times,
ZWING... ZWING... ZWING...!!!

So there were twenty-one Krishnas in all,
including himself, the original. WOW!
Twenty-one Krishnas!

Then, like magic, each of the
twenty Krishna photocopies became one of
the calves.

They looked exactly like the original calves.
They had the same white skin, the same
brown spots and the same skinny tails.
They even had the same *MOOOO!* And
Krishna laughed. All the cows laughed, too.

Krishna then photocopied himself again!
ZWING... ZWING... ZWING...!!!

WOW! Twenty more Krishnas!

This time he became each of his friends.
Every friend had the same eyes, the same
nose and the same hair as the originals.
They even had the same voice. And Krishna
giggled. All the friends giggled,too.

The Krishna-calves looked like the real
calves, and the Krishna-friends looked like
his real friends. Nobody could tell they
were all really Krishna.

Now the new calves and the new friends went home just as they would every evening. Each friend went to his own house with his own calves.

The mothers were extra happy to see their little boys that day. Even the cows were extra happy to see their calves that day.

Nobody could understand why they were suddenly feeling more love for their children and calves.

They did not understand what was happening.

But we know why, don't we?

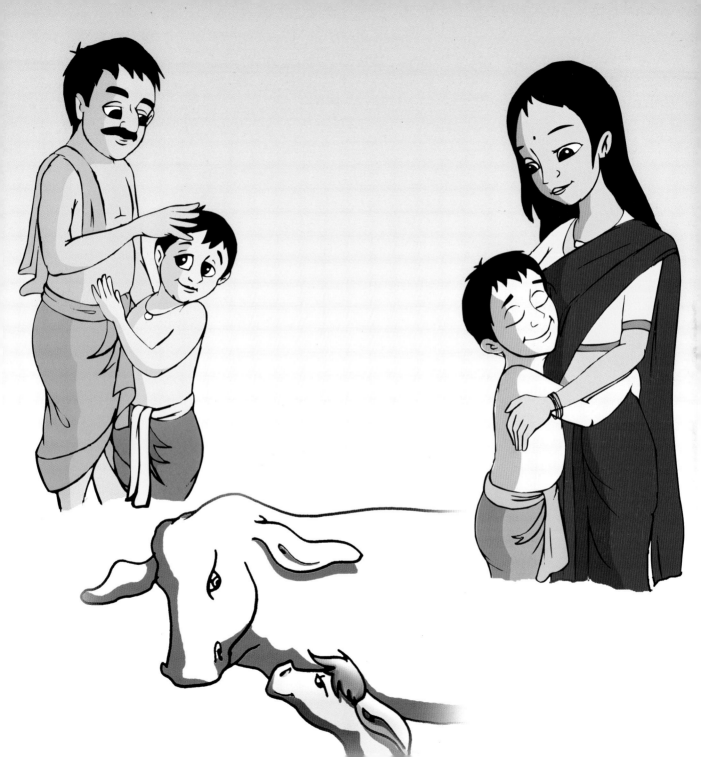

Now Brahma returned to the skies to see what was happening. He sat on his fluffy white cloud, stroking his long white beard.

He saw Krishna playing with all his friends! And he saw all the calves munching on lovely green grass!

He was surprised. He rubbed his eyes and looked again.

"What? How can this be? How can Krishna's friends and their calves all be here, when I hid them in the cave?"

He was confused.

So he rushed to the cave. He saw all of Krishna's friends and all their calves sound asleep, just the way he had left them.

Brahma was VERY confused.

"How can the boys be sleeping here and also playing with Krishna in the forest? How can it be?"

So he went back to the forest to look again.

Now Krishna was watching Brahma's puzzled face. "Ah, he has only hidden the cows, but I have hidden myself!

"**He sees the cows, but he does not see me. He sees my friends, but he does not see me,**" said Krishna to himself, now tickled deep blue.

Then Krishna used his magic to show Brahma the truth:

While Brahma was looking down at all the friends playing with Krishna, he saw each friend turn into Krishna.

But how could this be?

One by one, the photocopied Krishna-friends turned back into Krishna.

Brahma's eyes become wide, and his mouth fell open. He could not believe what he was seeing!

He then looked at the calves, and saw each calf turn into Krishna. One by one, the photocopied Krishna-calves turned back into Krishna.

Everyone Brahma looked at was Krishna. Everything he looked at was Krishna. Everywhere he looked, there was Krishna. Krishna! Krishna! **Krishna!**

"Oh, no!" thought Brahma. He knew he had made a mistake, a BIG mistake.

He quickly went to Krishna and said, "I am sorry, I am very sorry. Please forgive me. I thought I was wise, but I am really otherwise. I wanted to show you how powerful I am. But you are greater than me. You are the greatest and wisest."

Brahma now knew Krishna was the best. Krishna was so kind and loving, and so wise.

Krishna photocopied himself and changed himself.

Which means, Krishna can become anyone and everyone, and we might not recognize him.

We could even be meeting Krishna every day... and not know it!

Maybe he became the friends you play with.

Maybe he became your mum and dad.

Maybe he became your teacher at school.